the Pagemaster™

CLASSIC SERIES

GULLIVER'S TRAVELS

Adapted from the novel by Jonathan Swift

the Pagemaster™
CLASSIC SERIES

GULLIVER'S TRAVELS

Adapted by	Illustrated by
Andrew Borkowski	**Tom Taylor**

the Pagemaster™ Classic Series was inspired by the Pagemaster™, a feature film presented by Twentieth Century Fox in association with Turner Pictures. TM & © 1994 Twentieth Century Fox Film Corporation and Turner Pictures, Inc. All rights reserved. Gulliver's Travels adaptation: Text copyright and illustration copyright © 1994 Tribute Publishing Inc. Published in Canada by Tribute Publishing Inc., Don Mills, Ontario. Printed in Canada by Quebecor.   ISBN 1-896298-04-4

the Pagemaster™

presents

GULLIVER'S TRAVELS

Adapted from the novel by Jonathan Swift

My name is Lemuel Gulliver. For most of my working life, I have been at sea, beginning as a ship's doctor. I had been the surgeon aboard a number of vessels and travelled to many strange lands before joining the crew of the *Antelope* on the fourth of May, 1699.

As we set sail for the Dutch East Indies, I had no idea that I was embarking on one of the strangest voyages ever undertaken by an Englishman! All went well on our trip until, somewhere near Tasmania, a violent typhoon overtook us. It was too much for our poor ship, which was caught up in the storm and sank.

I was lucky enough to be one of

six men who managed to climb aboard a lifeboat, but, soon enough, the gigantic waves over-

get myself free. As soon as the threads began to loosen, the little men pro-duced tiny bows

powered the tiny craft and we were tossed headlong into the sea.

I swam for what seemed to be many miles until the seas grew calm and an island came into view. About a mile from shore, the water suddenly became shallow enough for me to walk the rest of the way to the beach where, exhausted, I collapsed and fell into a deep sleep.

When I awoke, I found myself unable to move. My arms, my legs, even my hair, had been tied to the ground with hundreds of tiny threads. Surrounding me was an army of men who were no more than six inches high! I was so shocked by the sight that I automatically began to struggle to

and I was showered with arrows that stung like the bites of a thousand insects. Then a tower was built near my face and the leader of the group climbed on top of it.

"Langro dehulsan!" he shouted. Then he gave a long speech, which I could not understand. My only answer to him was to point to my mouth to show him that I was hungry. Ladders were put up my sides and the little men brought me all kinds of delicious meats to eat and wine to drink. I decided that I could not hurt people who had been so kind to me. But I soon found out that the wine had been drugged and I fell asleep.

When I woke up, I had been

tied to a wagon that was being pulled by 1,500 tiny horses. The little men danced round my ears, shouting and signalling. I was already able to understand enough of their language to know that their island was called Lilliput, and that these Lilliputians were taking me to the city of Mildendo to meet their King.

The King seemed like a good man. His subjects had many long names for him, like "monarch of monarchs," and "His most sublime majesty." The big names suited him because he was a big man, standing almost half a fingernail taller than any of his subjects.

Teachers were brought to teach me the Lilliputian language and as soon as I knew enough to speak with the King, I asked him for my freedom.

He was unwilling to grant it, but seemed eager to make me happy and comfortable in every other way. I was given hundreds of servants and all the citizens of Lilliput were ordered to do everything to look after my needs. Special shows were put on in my honour. I particularly liked some of the Lilliputian dances. There was one in which subjects stood on a tightrope and competed to see who could jump the highest without falling.

In another dance, the courtiers jumped over or crawled under a pole held by the King himself. Hoping for my freedom, I thought it wise to do my part to amuse the King and his subjects. Once, I tied my handkerchief to four sticks

and made a stage on which the Lilliputian army could perform their drills for all to see. Another time, I stood with my feet apart, making a kind of magnificent archway of myself through which the army passed in a special parade (though some of the soldiers laughed when, looking up, they were able to see through the holes in the seat of my pants!).

The King's cavalry also enjoyed using my hands and feet as obstacles to jump over so they could show off their riding skills. It was important to give the Lilliputians this kind of pleasure, because I knew my situation was not without some danger. There were some people in the court who would have liked to see me dead. They said that the cost of feeding the "man-mountain," as they had come to call me, would cause famine and starvation in the rest of the land. Flimnap, the King's treasurer, even recommended that I be poisoned, or be allowed to starve to death.

So I took every opportunity to show my good will. At the same time, I took care to gently suggest that, if threatened, I was capable of doing them great harm. For example, at one point, the men who had shot arrows at me on my first day in Lilliput were brought before me. The King said I was free to give them whatever punishment I wanted. Knowing this was a test, I forgave the men but not without pointing out that I could always eat them if I wanted to.

I was also happy when the King asked me to show what I could do with my weapons. The sight of my sword glinting in the sun and the loud "BANG!" of my pistol frightened the little people nearly to death. I knew that it was by serving the King and his people that I would find the best way to regain my freedom, and there was no better way to serve the King than by helping him in his war against the Emperor of Blefuscu in the matter of the Big Endians and the Little Endians.

Long ago, the King of Lilliput's grandfather had decreed that Lilliputians who broke open their boiled eggs at the big end, instead of the little end, would be sent to prison. Those who refused to obey the law were called Big Endians and sent into exile on Blefuscu, the island next to Lilliput. The Emperor of Blefuscu was himself

a believer in Big Endianism and declared war on the Little Endians. He had now assembled a huge fleet and was ready to invade Lilliput at any moment.

Here was my chance to win the undying gratitude of the Lilliputians and my freedom. Taking a spool of thread and the box of fishhooks I had managed to save from the wreck of the *Antelope,* I made 50 cables with hooks on the end. I then waded across the channel separating the two islands and attached the cables to the 50 warships I found anchored off Blefuscu.

This was no easy task. The army of Blefuscu bravely tried to stop me from stealing their fleet, bombarding me with thousands of stinging little arrows as I worked.

But I had the foresight to bring my glasses which protected my eyes and enabled me to finish the job and drag the Blefuscudian fleet back to Lilliput in triumph. Instantly, I became the country's greatest hero and the King suggested more ways in which I could be of help to him against the Emperor of Blefuscu.

"Now man-mountain," he said, "you must return to Blefuscu and capture the Emperor's merchant ships as well. Then the Blefuscudians will have no choice but to surrender to us and become our slaves, and I shall be emperor of all the known world."

"With respect your majesty," I told him, "the Blefuscudians are a brave and free people. I would never allow myself to bring them into slavery."

Everything I had seen in Lilliput — its laws, the beauty of its gardens, the playfulness of its people — had lead me to believe it a good and fair country. I now saw it as my job to make peace for them with their neighbours, a good and lasting peace. I met with ambassadors from Blefuscu and agreed to travel there to speak with the Emperor and see what kind of arrangements might be possible.

But it was not to be. The King had said nothing to me, but secretly he was angry that I had not done as he had asked. Now Flimnap, the treasurer, began to conspire against me and soon I found out, through a friend, that I had secretly been charged with treason. Calling me a traitor, Flimnap demanded "the most painful death" for me. My friend at court, Reldresal, suggested that it would be enough if the King had me blinded instead of killed. Flimnap disagreed with this saying that blinding the man-mountain would only make him eat more, the way blinded chickens do, and cause a famine in the land.

Finally, the King agreed that I should be blinded. In three days, my friend told me, Reldresal would come to me and read the charges. He would be followed by 20 Lilliputian doctors who were to take out my eyes.

I wondered what to do. Certainly someone of my size could have destroyed the whole kingdom with a stroke of my hand. It was tempting to wait and fight the ridiculous charges against me. But I had come to realize that the cunning of the Lilliputians knew no bounds. The longer I waited, whether it was to fight, or to argue my case, the greater the danger I was in.

Then I remembered the friends I had made in Blefuscu because of my refusal to completely destroy their ships and make slaves of them. I decided to escape there, wading across the channel once again to find the Emperor welcoming me with open arms.

Upon learning of my escape, the King of Lilliput immediately demanded that I be sent back to his island to face my punishment. The Emperor refused to do so, and he suggested that, in return for his protection, I should serve him as I had once served the Lilliputians. Politely, I refused. I knew better now than to trust kings and emperors. All I could think of was to return home, to be once again among people like myself.

A few days afterwards, I came across a life boat of normal human size that had blown ashore after a storm. I dragged it to safety and began preparing it for the voyage home.

The Blefuscudians were of great help to me in fixing up the boat. They gladly gave me enough food and water to last many days at sea. They also gave me some of their tiny cows and sheep which I hoped to raise once I returned to England. When I finally set off from that strange corner of the world, I could tell that the people of Blefuscu were glad to see me go.

I rowed out to sea not knowing where I was going or if I would survive. Certainly my small boat would never have taken me all the way to England. But I was lucky. A very short while after I left Blefuscu, I was spotted and taken aboard an English merchant ship. I told the ship's captain my whole story, and I think he thought me a madman until I showed him the miniature animals I had brought with me from Blefuscu.

I returned to England on April 13, 1702, almost three years after I had left. The souvenirs I brought home from Blefuscu soon made me a wealthy man. Lords and ladies were willing to pay large amounts of money just to see my miniature animals.

A VOYAGE TO BROBDINGNAG

I grew bored after only two months back in England. Once again I heeded the call of the sea and, on the 20th of June, 1702, I set sail on the *Adventure*, which was bound for Surat.

We had been at sea for almost a year when, east of Molucca, the ship was struck by two huge storms, one after the other. This time our ship did not sink, but the storms blew us so far off course that, by the time fair weather returned, we had no idea where we were. Then, on June 16, 1703, a vast uncharted body of land appeared on the horizon.

Once we were close enough to this body of land, myself and a small group of men set out for it in a small boat. We went ashore to look for water, but I could not resist exploring a little of this unknown place. I spied a hill not far from the beach where we landed and climbed it hoping to get a better look at the surrounding countryside. I got to the top of the hill just in time to see my fellow sailors rowing furiously out to sea.

They were being chased by a giant, a monstrous man no less than 70 feet high! If it hadn't been for a series of huge, jagged rocks at the mouth of the bay we had entered, they would have been finished. But my fellow crewmen managed to slip through the rocks, while the giant, afraid of cutting his bare feet on the sharp rocks, gave up the chase.

Stranded, I knew I had to find some place to hide in case there were more of these giants around. After wandering inland, I found a field of corn. But this was no ordinary corn. The stalks were easily 40 feet high! I thought it would be a good hiding place at least until night when I might return to the beach in the hope that my shipmates would try to rescue me under cover of darkness.

It wasn't to be. I waited a couple of hours then I heard a great swooping sound, followed by a deafening crack and crunching noises. Peering out between the stalks, I spied seven monsters just like the one that had chased my sailor friends from the beach. They carried huge scythes which they were using to cut down the corn stalks. They were coming closer and closer, the sharp shining blades slicing away stalks as thick as oak trees at a single powerful stroke.

Rather than let myself be cut to pieces, I decided to give myself up. I stepped out into the blazing sun and immediately fell into the shadow of one of the monsters. Seeing me, the giant uttered a puzzled grunt which, to my ears, sounded like the roar of a bear or lion.

He bent over and picked me up between his fingers, as if he was afraid that I might bite or sting him. He then placed me in the open palm of another man who seemed to be his master. This man, after a bit of poking and prodding which bruised my ribs, closed his fingers gently over me and carried me away.

Between his fingers I could see what would have passed for a small cottage in this country, but it was at least 200 feet high. The giant took me inside this house and placed me on the table which was set for supper. There I sat as the family of giants ate their meal, talking amongst themselves and guessing what kind of creature I might be.

Their voices were so loud I could hardly hear myself think. When I tried to shout to them they couldn't hear a word of what I said. There were so many dangers around me that I very nearly met my death several times during that meal.

First, the farmer's little boy picked me up and swung me around by the legs, almost pulling them off.

Next, a cat the size of an ox jumped up onto the table and would certainly have snatched me up in its jaws and eaten me whole if the farmer had not quickly thrown it from the table.

Then the baby grabbed me and put my head into its mouth. Before it could suck the head right off of my shoulders, I let out as ferocious a roar as I could. The noise succeeded in frightening the baby so that it dropped me into its toys and cried so much it had to be picked up in order to calm it.

My final close call of the afternoon came after the farmer's wife had set me down to rest on a bed that was 20 yards wide and eight yards high. The pillows on this bed rose up like mountains and the quilt covering was soft as soft can be. The bedroom was 300 feet wide and at least 200 feet high.

No sooner had I settled in for a

sleep than I was attacked by two rats. I was able to kill one of them with my sword and wound the other one as it ran away. I measured the tail of the dead rat. It was six feet long.

I realized the strange position my new adventure put me in. It was the exact opposite of the way things had been on my last voyage, in Lilliput. Where once it was I who was the giant, now it was I

who was to be the "Lilliputian" among this race of men-mountains. Looking at my new masters made me think of how those tiny people I had encountered in my last adventure must have felt when they were with me.

The giants seemed horribly ugly to me. Everything about them was magnified for my eyes. On these huge creatures, a simple freckle or mole could look the size of a dinner plate sprouting hairs that looked like thick black wires. The hair on their heads was like rope and when they sneezed, oh boy, watch out! Up close, their skins seemed to be covered in spots and pimples. Then I remembered how the Lilliputians had once told me that my skin was full of huge black holes.

I also remembered the time a Lilliputian friend told me how much I stank. I now knew what he had meant. These enormous people, who I learned were called Brobdingnagians, gave off smells that they didn't seem to notice but to my nose were the worst odours I had ever encountered.

Much worse were the perfumes on the ladies I would later meet in Brobdingnag. These were so awful they made me faint. I became a combination toy and pet to the farmer's 10-year-old daughter, and we soon became good friends. She washed me and made clothes for me and taught me how to speak her language. She called me Grildig, which was Brobding-nagian for "little man." I named her Glumdalclitch, which meant "little nurse."

But Glumdalclitch's father got the idea of taking me into the town and putting me on display for anyone curious enough to pay. From then on I was bundled into a box and carried to market every day where I was forced to wave my sword, show myself off and per-form stunts to amuse the paying customers.

Soon we were touring the markets in all the towns of Brobdingnag and I was perform-ing as many as 10 times a day. By the time we reached the capital city of Lorbrulgrud, I was nothing but skin and bones. My master was certain that I would soon die of exhaustion and was only too glad to sell me to the Queen of Brobdingnag for a great price.

Luckily my beloved Glumdal-clitch was allowed to come to the palace with me. She was put in charge of my care and a special house was ordered built for me to live in.

The royal family were very fond of me and I was invited to dine with them every day. At meals, the King was very interested in hear-ing about our English schools, laws, religions, and government. But when I told him about these things, he only laughed and called us Englishmen "little insects."

The Brobdingnagians began to make me think of myself as being much smaller than I really was. I began thinking about people back in England as if they were Lilliputians, tiny people walking around with their chests all puffed out, thinking they were much more important than they really were.

There were still plenty of people and things to scare and torture me at the court. The Queen's dwarf, who was only 30 feet high, was delighted to find someone smaller than he was. He loved to pick on me. Once, when he was angry at me, he shook the apple tree I was sitting under and I was almost killed by falling apples as big as barrels.

Another day I was attacked by 20 huge wasps. I managed to kill four of them and chased the

others away with my sword. Then a monkey grabbed me and took me up to the palace roof. It seems the animal thought I was one of its babies and it tried to stuff my mouth full of mushed bananas. Everyone at court laughed at me after this last adventure.

The palace was such a gigantic place. It measured seven miles across and the kitchen alone was 600 feet high. It made me feel very sad to see how small and unimportant I was compared with everything around me. To cheer me up, the Queen, who knew how much I loved the sea, had a

tiny boat built for me.

The workmen also built a wooden box that was 300 feet long, 50 feet wide and eight feet deep. When they filled the box with water I was able to put on shows of my rowing and sailing abilities for the Queen and her ladies. Sometimes the ladies would help by making powerful winds for me with their fans.

I was so eager to please my masters, I tried making things for myself that would amuse them like a miniature comb from the shavings of the King's beard. I even invented a

way of playing their piano by running up and down the keyboard whacking on the keys with two giant poles.

When I found out that there was no such thing as gunpowder in Brobdingnag, I told the King all about it. I told him how it could destroy whole armies, sink ships manned by a thousand men and flatten entire cities. But when I offered to make the King some gunpowder he was horrified.

"Anyone who would invent such a terrible thing," he thundered, "is the enemy of all mankind! How could a little insect like you entertain such beastly notions? I would rather lose half my kingdom than share in your secret. If I find that you have told anyone else about this horrible invention, I will have you crushed like the bug you are!"

With that, I gave up all hope of ever gaining the respect of the Brobdingnagians. I seemed doomed to remain their toy for the rest of my life and I was horrified when the King suggested that he capture an English ship to find me a wife so that we could make children to be curiosities for all the people of his realm.

I had been in Brobdingnag for two years when the King and Queen decided to take me on a trip to the seashore. While we were there, a page was ordered to take me outside in my house, to give me some fresh air. The sea air soon made me drowsy and the page, thinking I was asleep, set me down in the dunes and went off to pick some apples. I did fall asleep and when I woke up, I found myself, still in the box, but bobbing and weaving several hundred feet in the air. The box had been grabbed by an eagle and it was taking me out to sea. Finally the eagle dropped me into the ocean where I stayed afloat long enough to be picked up by a passing English merchant ship. I made the trip safely back to England and returned to the loving arms of my wife and daughter.

A VOYAGE TO LAPUTA, BALNIBARBI, LUGGNAGG, GLUBBDUBRIB AND JAPAN

My reputation as a sailor and adventurer had grown and I was made a captain and put in charge of a small trading ship which sailed off the coast of China. In 1706, my ship was travelling one of its regular routes when it was captured by pirates. The pirates took charge of the ship and my crew were made prisoners. They put me in a lifeboat and set me adrift with only enough food and water for eight days. On the fifth day I sighted a small group of islands and went ashore on one of them.

The island seemed deserted and I spent a night taking shelter in a cave worrying, that with no one around to help, I might well die here. The next morning I stepped out into the sunshine, only to find that the sky had suddenly gone completely dark. A huge round disc in the sky had blotted out the sun. It was a flying island, floating above me about two miles up in the air. I got out my telescope for a better look. I could see that its bottom was perfectly flat and smooth, and it shone with the reflection of the sea. It was a frightening sight, but I was delighted to see people walking on it. Rescue was at hand!

The island moved around the sky, up and down, backwards and forwards, as if someone were controlling it. When it came close, I could see buildings with many levels, all connected by stairs. On the very lowest part of the island there were people fishing. I shouted and waved to these people and the island came down to a point about 100 yards above my head. A kind of swing was lowered to me. I got on it and they pulled me up.

A huge crowd of people were waiting for me. They all looked the same. Their heads were tilted to one side and they each had one eye turned completely inwards while the other eye stared straight up into the sky. Every person had a servant standing next to them. The servants carried short sticks with small balloons attached to the end. Inside the balloons were dried peas or pebbles. Once in a while, each servant would turn to his master and smack him on some part of the face with the balloon.

Later on, I learned that the people of this island, which was called Laputa, were so busy thinking that they had to be smacked in the mouth to remind them to speak. When someone spoke to them, it took a smack on the ears to get them to listen. From time to time, they even had to be slapped in order to make them watch where they were going.

The crowd took me to the royal palace which was at the very highest part of the island. This took some time because my guides forgot what they were doing several times along the way. They had to be reminded by their servants, or "flappers," who would tap their brains in order to help them remember where they were going.

Inside the palace I was taken to the King's throne room which was filled with globes, triangles, rulers, compasses and all kinds of mathematical equipment. The King did not notice me. Instead, he sat staring into space for almost an hour, as if he were thinking very hard about some problem. When he did start to speak, I was immediately slapped on the ear by one of the flappers. I told him that I had no need of smacking. That made all the others in the room think that I must be very stupid if my thoughts were not deep enough to need a slap to bring me back to reality.

Unfortunately I wasn't able to understand the King until a few

days later, when I had managed to learn the Laputan language. While I was studying, I learned about some of the odd customs on this strange island.

Everything in their society was based on mathematical or musical principles. So, when a beautiful woman passed, someone might say, "Just look at the parallelograms on that woman!"

"Such fine rectangles!" another might say. Someone who knew her might speak even of her pianissimo temperament.

I noticed that, in spite of their love of thinking and mathematics, there was not much good work being done. I was measured for a new set of clothes. My tailor measured me from head to foot and from stem to stern with compasses and rulers and made long scientific calculations as he did so. Unfortunately, seven days later, the clothes were delivered to me badly made and in the wrong shape because he had made a mistake in all his adding and subtracting.

As a matter of fact, the Laputans did not like the idea of using their knowledge in order to actually do anything. Their houses were as badly made as their clothes. They lived only for science and music and their language did not even contain the necessary words that would enable them to talk intelligently about anything else.

It was true that they were also very good at astronomy. They knew far more about the stars and the planets than anyone in Europe. But it was a knowledge about things they couldn't control, so they were always worried about some impending disaster in the heavens and were often unable to sleep.

The King had incredible power over the people who lived on the land below his floating island. He could use the island to stop sunshine and rain from falling on the lands of his enemies. He could even land it on the ground and crush everything underneath it if he wanted. But he never did. Too many of his lords had land below and they would never have allowed it.

In truth, nothing much happened on the flying island of Laputa. The men were too busy walking around with their heads in the clouds, always thinking, never doing. So I was glad to get permission to leave after only two months. I got that permission with help from a friend at court. This friend was a man who had done great work for the kingdom, who paid attention when he was spoken to and only used a flapper on public holidays. He was a failure at mathematics, however, and many at court laughed at him behind his back.

The land beneath Laputa was called Balnibarbi. I was dropped into its capital city, Lagado. There I met one of the local Lords, a man named Munodi. His lands were green and rich and very different from the rest of the country. Everywhere I looked, I saw people working hard in the fields from dawn to dusk, but they had little to show for it.

For the most part, these people were poor, ragged and sickly. Munodi told me that the reason he was so successful was that he had not taken up the new farming methods. These methods had been developed at the Academy of Projectors in Lagado. The Projectors were businessmen who had learned a bit about Laputan mathematics while visiting the flying island. Believing they had become expert scientists, they returned and set up their academy.

The Projectors invented ways of building and farming that were supposed to allow one man to do the work of 10. They had schemes to make and grow a hundred times more vegetables, or to enable people to build palaces in a week that would last forever. But none of these schemes worked and the country was in ruins.

People hated Munodi because he had not followed the advice of the Projectors and stayed quite wealthy. Whenever one of the new projects failed, neighbours did their best to find a way of putting the blame on him.

He had once owned a mill that was very prosperous. The Projectors took it over and, instead of using water from the river right next to the mill in order to turn it, they invented a plan to pump water up a nearby mountain and create a waterfall to do the job. One hundred men worked on the mill for two years, but, of course, the plan could never work. The project was abandoned. Seven years later the mill was still

a wreck and the local people still blamed Munodi for it.

I decided that the Academy of Lagado had to be seen to be believed, so I arranged to visit it as soon as I could. The warden gave me a warm welcome and only too happily gave me a tour of its 500 rooms. There were projects to get sunshine out of cucumbers, to build houses from the roof down the way spiders and bees do, to make gunpowder by heating ice and to plough fields by planting acorns so that pigs would root them up and dig furrows in the process.

Some of the professors were inventing a new language in which people talked, not in words, but by showing each other things. You could see these professors, from time to time, in the streets of Lagado. They walked around with huge packs on their backs stuffed with objects. When they met one another they would take off their backpacks and spend hours "talking" by showing each other their things.

At the mathematics school of the academy, students were trying to learn how to solve problems by eating cookies with the answers written on them. So far, the experiment wasn't working. What was even more interesting were some of the Academy's ideas about government. One professor said that the best way to stop politicians from fighting one another was to take out their brains and chop them in half. Doctors could then take half of the brains of one group of leaders and sew them onto the half-brains of another group of leaders. That way all the leaders would think the same and there would be no more arguing.

I had seen and heard enough and I decided to go to the neighbouring island of Luggnagg. There I was told by the local seamen about the amazing things that could be seen on the next island in the chain, Glubbdubdrib. It was a place entirely run by sorcerers and magicians.

I got the first boat at hand to ferry me across to Glubbdubdrib and went directly to the palace of the governor. The governor had the power to command the dead and the mansion was teeming with ghosts. All his servants were spirits, so ashen-faced and ghoulish that they made my skin crawl. But I got used to them in a couple of days and I was happy to take the governor up on his offer to summon up any spirit I might like to meet from the land of the dead.

At first I was delighted to meet some of the greatest philosophers, poets, and leaders in the history of mankind. But many of the things I learned from them saddened me too. They made clear to me that much of what I had been taught about them in history classes were lies.

What I found saddest of all was how great these men seemed in comparison to the thinkers and leaders of my own time. Hoping at least to find some noble ancestors for the great leaders of England, I had the governor summon up the ghosts of their families. Instead I was distressed to learn that some of our mightiest noblemen were actually the descendants of thieves and liars.

I went back to Luggnagg where I learned there was one last set of wonders to see on these unusual islands. These were the Stuldbruggs, people who had been born with a red circle on their foreheads. The red marks told their families that these children would never die. They were immortal.

"Happy nation," I thought, "to be blessed with so much ancient wisdom to guide them."

I quickly learned that to live for-ever was no blessing at all, neither for the people of Luggnagg nor for the Stuldbruggs themselves. Often they would look enviously at a passing funeral, wishing that they might die before becoming like older Stuldbruggs. It was true that they did not die once they reached a normal old age. Instead their bodies turned into a kind of pud-ding and their minds disintegrated to the point where they could remember nothing, not even the words of the simplest sentence. And that was how they were to doomed to sit, alive but lifeless, for all eternity.

Because this place was so close to Japan, I thought I might try to make a visit to that country. So I went to the King of Luggnagg for a letter of introduction to the Emperor of Japan.

Getting this kind of favour was a tricky business. I had to send the necessary note to His Majesty of Luggnagg asking for the honour of licking up the dust in front of His royal footstool. The King granted me an audience, but when I arrived at court, I was very surprised to learn that I was expected to do exactly what the note had said. On entering the royal chamber I was ordered to lie down on the floor and crawl on my belly towards the throne, lick-ing the floor as I went.

I was lucky. Being a stranger to the kingdom, the floor was cleaned for me. Others who had enemies at court often found the floor covered with extra dirt when it was their turn to approach the King.

The King granted me my letter to the Japanese Emperor, but I did not stay long in Japan. I booked a passage to Amsterdam on the *Amboyna*. The ship arrived safely and I continued on to England and my family. I had been away five years and six months.

A VOYAGE TO THE COUNTRY OF THE HOUYHNHNMS

After five months at home, I was lured away to sea again, this time as captain of a 350 ton merchant ship bound for the West Indies. During the voyage a number of our sailors died and I had to put ashore to take on new crewmen. It turned out that these new men were pirates in disguise.

As soon as we were at sea again, they took control of the ship. I was bound in chains and kept locked in my cabin for many days. At last they rowed me to an island and left me with no idea of where I was.

There was no sign of any human life on the island, but I soon noticed monkey-like animals lurking in the forest beyond the shore. They were terribly ugly, with thick hanks of matted hair on some parts of their bodies while other parts showed skin that was dark with filth. They had no tails but, with their long claws, they could climb trees as quickly and easily as squirrels.

I kept my distance from these animals, but it wasn't long before one of them approached me as I walked along a road. The creature stared at me rudely, then began waving his filthy paws in my face. I slapped him across the arm with the flat of my sword. The animal gave out a howl that brought 40 of the creatures down on me. They surrounded me, screeching and making horrible faces. Some of them climbed up on the trees and showered me with all kinds of dirt. I was just getting ready to defend myself with my sword when the animals suddenly disappeared.

I was left standing face to face with a horse. The horse looked me up and down, his eyes wide with wonder. I tried to move away from him several times but, each time, he blocked my way and gently nudged me back to my place under a tree. When I tried to pat the horse, he shook his head at me and brushed my hand away with one of his front feet.

Another horse came along. The two animals bowed to one another and began making a series of snorts and whinnies that, if I hadn't known better, I might have taken for conversation. They did seem to be talking about me, as I gathered from the way they kept looking at me and shaking their heads in my direction.

They came up to me again and inspected me all over with their snouts. Hoping they might be magicians in disguise, I asked them if they could give me a ride to the nearest town. The horses blinked in surprise and again began talking to one another. I was able to make out a word that they repeated several times — "Yahoo." I turned to the horses and said "Yahoo" in as clear a voice as I could muster. They looked very surprised, then repeated it a few more times, apparently so I could learn exactly how it was pronounced.

Then they taught me another word, "Houyhnhnm," which was pronounced "whinnum." They seemed amazed that I could learn these words so quickly. The second horse bowed to the first and went on his way.

The first horse then turned to me and, with a whinny and a shake of his neck, signalled that I should follow him. That I did for about three miles. Then we came to a low house made of tree trunks stuck in the ground with a straw roof.

We entered a room with a clay floor in which five other horses were standing. My guide neighed sharply at them, as if he were giving them instructions, then took me to wait in another room. He then went back to the first room and I overheard an exchange of snuffles and burring sounds that I now couldn't help but identify as whispered conversation.

I began to be afraid I was going out of my mind for believing that horses could talk. I even pinched myself to see if I was dreaming. Finally the horse that had brought me here returned and lead me into a third room. There I was presented with a mare, a colt, and a newborn foal, all lying on straw mats.

Once again I was inspected from head to toe and the three new horses kept repeating the word "yahoo" over and over. Then they took me outside and brought over a creature exactly like the filthy beasts that had attacked me earlier. I realized instantly that "Yahoo" was the name the horses called these creatures. The other word I had been taught, "Houyhnhnm," was the name the horses gave to themselves.

I was horrified when I realized the horses were comparing me to the dirty animal. I was even more horrified when I looked at the dirty animal and had to admit to myself that there were similarities. Aside from the mats of hair on his body, the smashed-in look of his face and the long, thick fingernails, the creature looked perfectly human!

The horses kept nudging and nipping at my clothes. It seemed

that my clothing confused them because it made my body look different from that of other Yahoos. They were surprised when I refused to eat the stinking mash that served as Yahoo-food. When they brought me oats and hay instead, I really began to think I would starve to death on this island. Finally, by mooing and pulling at an imaginary udder, I was able to make them understand that I would drink cow's milk. They brought me some, and I was allowed to drink to my heart's content.

That evening, an older horse came for dinner, pulling up in a sledge dragged by four Yahoos. I sat in a corner as the master horse, his family and their guests, carefully nibbled at their hay and made a series of low neighs in my direction. The old horse seemed very interested in my gloves. I showed him how I could take them off and stuff them in my pockets. The horses whinnied with glee when they saw this and, as a reward, they taught me a few more words of their language.

It was hard work, but I learned the Houyhnhnm language, which reminded me of Dutch or German. The master horse and all the others insisted on calling me a Yahoo, but they were clearly confused by my ability to learn, by my good manners, and by how clean I kept myself.

The thing that made me most different from the Yahoos, in the horses' minds, was the fact that I wore clothes. They didn't realize that I could take them off until one morning a servant came into my lodge and found me sleeping naked. The master was surprised that anyone would want to cover their body, but he allowed me to keep my underpants on while he and his servants looked me over one more time.

With the mystery of my clothing solved, some of the horses were now ready to think of me as a Yahoo, while others thought that the name wasn't quite right for me. After all, I had shown that I could speak and think, my skin was almost hairless, and I could walk upright (though the master Houyhnhnms thought I did this out of sheer silliness).

I begged the master to stop calling me a Yahoo and tried to explain to him that every other country in the world was controlled by creatures just like me. When he said he could not believe that was true, I went even further. I made him promise not to be angry with me for telling him what I was about to tell him.

Then I described how, in other countries, horses were treated as dumb animals. I told him how, in England, they were used to pull wagons and coaches, how men rode upon their backs and taught them to race and jump fences for their amusement.

The master horse was completely astonished that such things could happen. I soon learned that the Houyhnhnms were the most reasonable people on earth. They had only the most noble emotions, and didn't know how to be angry, or jealous. Because they were so reasonable, no one lied on this island. Their language didn't even have a word for lying.

That made it very difficult for them when I began to tell my tales of England, a country ruled by Yahoos. They couldn't believe I was lying because they didn't know what a lie was. At the same time, they couldn't believe the things I told them because they couldn't imagine anything that they hadn't seen for themselves.

Nevertheless they listened with interest as I told them about our courts in which lawyers were paid to prove that black is white and white is black in front of judges who had grown fat and lazy. They had some problem understanding the concept of money and how it made a few people more rich and powerful than everyone else.

They whinnied out loud when I described how ships had to be sent all over the world to get tea and oranges and fancy china cups for a rich woman's breakfast. It seemed incredible to them that we should choose people who were raised in luxury and schooled in laziness to be our noblemen.

My account of how men drank wine, not as a replacement for water but to make them giddy from being out of their senses, met with snorts of disgust.

It was my description of war that horrified the Houyhnhnms the most. After I had told him about the horrors that took place in your average European war, my master ordered me to stop my tale in case he should become corrupted just by hearing about such horrors.

The Houyhnhnms were such a fine and decent race of beings, that I now saw how evil we humans are in comparison to them. I decided never to return home and to stay here for the rest of my days. There was nothing here to remind me about all the bad things that men said and did at home, except for the behaviour of the local Yahoos. I asked for permission to go out and study these creatures.

Up close to them in their stables, I coughed and spluttered at the stink of the Yahoos. Their actions were just as disgusting as their smell. They were greedy and hated each other because each one of them wanted everything to himself.

Stealing was seen as a good thing among them, and every Yahoo seemed to prize those things they had stolen over anything they had won by honest work.

The Yahoos didn't have any kind of government. Each band did have a leader who would choose an assistant. The assistant was usually the ugliest and most evil member of the band. His main job was to follow the leader around licking his feet. The rest of an assistant's energy went into keeping his job, because there was always someone uglier and more cruel and evil trying to take his place.

I began to see so many similarities between my own people and the Yahoos that I had to run away from them and promise myself never to go near them again. Secretly, I worried that the Houyhnhnms were right, that I really was a Yahoo, especially after one of the Yahoo women decided that I was handsome and tried to kiss me.

In spite of these fears, I became very happy in my life among the horses. It was a simple life that taught me how little I really needed to be satisfied.

I enjoyed perfect health and peace of mind. I had grown to love the reasonable talk of the horses, their gentle whinnies, their soft puffing and snorting. Their conversation was a kind of music to me, and I spoke only when asked something in case I should have to stop listening to their words while I was speaking.

My happiness didn't last, however. One day I received a terrible message from the Houyhnhnm government. They had decided that I had to leave. Some members of the assembly were offended that my master was keeping a Yahoo and treating him as if he were a Houyhnhnm. At the same time, the councillors were afraid to send me to live with the local Yahoos because I obviously had more intelligence than them. They were afraid that I might try to use my intelligence to organize the Yahoos into robbing their farms.

I was sickened at the thought of having to return to my own people, but I agreed to leave. Over the next six weeks I built a canoe covered in Yahoo skins, and filled it with boiled rabbit meat and other supplies. I kissed my master's foot, and he was kind enough to raise his leg so that I didn't need to bend all the way to the ground. Then I sailed off towards an island about five leagues away.

It was my hope that the new island would have nobody on it, just enough food and water to keep me healthy for the rest of my life. It was not to be. As I approached the shore, a group of wild savages rushed out of the trees firing arrows at me. One of the arrows struck me in the knee. I turned back out to sea and spied a sail approaching from the horizon. The thought of being picked up and returned to civilization was even more terrifying than the savages, so I turned back to shore where I found a hiding place in the forest.

The ship dropped anchor just off the cove where I had hidden myself. A party of four men rowed ashore. While looking for water, they stumbled upon me and spoke to me in Portuguese. They looked at me as if I had gone mad when I told them about the Houyhnhnms and the Yahoos, and they laughed at the neighing sounds I made when I spoke.

I was taken aboard the ship and presented to the captain. He seemed like a good fellow but after three years among the Houyhnhnms I was not used to the smell of people. To my nose, he stank horribly. His words were as unpleasant sounding as the snarling of dogs and I refused to answer any of his questions. As soon as the ship had put to sea, I tried to jump overboard and drown myself rather than face life among civilized human beings again. The captain made me

promise not to try to kill myself again. I gave him my promise but spent the rest of the voyage shut in my cabin, keeping as far away from the crew as possible.

When we arrived in the Portuguese capital of Lisbon, the good captain took me to live with him. Terrified of whatever thieves and murderers might be lurking in the streets, I insisted on having the highest room in the Captain's house and on being lead backwards up the stairs in case some villain might try to attack me from behind. I refused to wear clothes that might have been touched by some European Yahoo. Even brand new suits had to be hung out to air for at least a day before I would put them on. The captain managed to get me out into the street for walks, but I could only do it after plugging my nose with herbs.

My host also persuaded me, after many arguments, that, as a man of honour, I should return home to my family. Although I love my family very much and missed them dearly, it still took me a while to get used to being back.

I did return home to my family and was happy to see them again. But I spend most of my time here in the stables among the horses who remind me so much of my beloved Houyhnhnms. I sleep here. I take my meals here. It is here, with the sound of their puffing and whinnying in my ears, that I have written this story about all that has happened to me in my travels.

You must believe me when I tell you that every word of my story is the absolute truth. The Houyhnhnms have taught me to love the truth above all other things. On good days, I can almost believe that I have actually become a Houyhnhnm, despite my horrible very Yahoo-like appearance.

At the very least, I can assure you that my time among them has made me incapable of telling a lie.

32